CRAFTY LLAMA

MIKE KERR • ILLUSTRATED BY RENATA LIWSKA

BLOOMSBURY
CHILDREN'S BOOKS
NEW YORK   LONDON   OXFORD   NEW DELHI   SYDNEY

It was a lovely, sunny day!

Llama knew there were so many things she ought to do:
chores, this, that, and whatever.

But...

...it was such a beautiful day that
she wanted to do something special.

Something lovely.

So Llama did what she did when she
needed to figure things out.
   Llama did a whole lot of thinking and still
didn't know exactly what to do with the day.
   She felt like the answer was sitting right in
front of her, but she just couldn't see it.

Llama's friend Raccoon stopped by.
"That looks like fun," said Raccoon. "Can I join you?"
"Of course!" said Llama.

Another friend stopped by and joined them.
And another.

Soon, lots of friends were making things.
Beaver stopped by, too, but he didn't join in.

He wasn't interested in making
something unless it was useful.

"This is very . . . crafty! But what is it for?" asked Beaver.

"Actually, I don't know," replied Llama.

She hadn't thought about whether what she was making was useful. She had just been having fun *making*. "What would you use it for?" she asked.

"Hmm..." Beaver thought about it.

He wasn't sure.

"How about . . . ," said Raccoon.

"Or maybe . . . ," said Pony.

"Or what about . . . ," said Rabbit.

None of the ideas felt right, or even possible. Or safe!

More friends stopped by to see what Llama was up to.

All of Llama's "thinking" meant she had a whole lot of knitting to share.

She had something to tame Lion's mane.

Something to carry Elephant's trunk.

Something for Turtle when he came out of his shell.

Llama had never imagined all her fun could be so useful!
"I guess if you have fun making something, others are
bound to enjoy it too," said Llama.

Soon it seemed everyone had a new, crafty something.

Everyone but Beaver.

So Beaver did what
he did when he needed
to figure things out.

Beaver did a whole
lot of thinking . . .

But he still didn't know how he could
make a knitted something useful.

BEAVER AT WORK

Llama and Beaver took a little break . . .

. . . which became a long break. With all Beaver's "thinking," he had made something special for everyone, too.

Llama had an idea. "I know what Beaver can use a crafty something for."

"Something special just for you!" Llama whispered. "Something lovely," murmured Beaver.

And Llama and her friends looked forward to spending
many more lovely days in a special, crafty, useful way.